THE LIBRARY OF AFRO CURIOSITIES

This book is a work of fiction. The names, characters, places and incidents are products of the author's imagination or have been used fictitiously and are not to be construed as real. Any resemblance to persons, living or dead, actual events, locales or organizations is entirely coincidental.

ISBN: 9781020001321 (Hardcover)
ISBN: 9781020001338 (Paperback)

First Edition

10 9 8 7 6 5 4 3 2

45 Alternate Press, LLC
Hampton, Virginia

Praise for Ran Walker

He's just that talented. To paraphrase Ethridge Knight: Making jazz swing in one hundred words AIN'T no square writer's job.

Rion Amilcar Scott, award-winning author of *Insurrections* and *The World Doesn't Require You*

I'm never quite at ease in a Ran Walker story. And that's a good thing. He's a master of the 100-word form.

Grant Faulkner, Executive Director of NaNoWriMo and Co-Founder of *100 Word Story*

Thank you, Ran, for picking up the guitar of fiction and fretting together characters of such warmth, depth, and humanity.

Tyehimba Jess, Pulitzer Prize-winning author of *Olio* and *Leadbelly*

Walker's clarity of style and smooth, mellifluous language [...] place him among the cadre of new Black voices budding with fresh, ripe tales of a past and present yet to unfold.

Ran Walker excels at cross-threading various genres into bite-sized, literary wonders.

THE LIBRARY OF AFRO CURIOSITIES

100-Word Stories

RAN WALKER

45 Alternate Press, LLC

Contents

In Memory of Sonia Russell

THE LIBRARY OF AFRO CURIOSITIES

They'll see how beautiful I am
    And be ashamed—

                    Langston Hughes

Planet 4C

PICK AND PAT. Pick and pat.

Doneisha's hands moved about Imani's seven-year-old head, taking the beautiful chaos of coiled hair and shaping it as the Creator might have once crafted the universe, her brown fingers moving like those of her mother and her mother's mother, liberating every strand to stand at its full potential.

"Mommy, is it done?"

"Almost."

"Please make it perfect."

The sphere gradually emerged, a celestial body born into their tiny sliver of the universe.

"Done."

Doneisha lifted the mirror to Imani's face, watching the reflection of her daughter's eyes, twin spheres filled with constellations of joy.

Cold

HE'D NEVER TOLD a girl that he loved her before. The anxiety was far worse than a first kiss, his teeth chattering as if he'd been blasted by cold air. Although the June night was hot, she rubbed his arms, to warm him.

He started a couple of times, the vibration of his teeth getting in the way. Finally, amid a sparse chorus of crickets and the buzz of the street lamp over head, he said the words.

She responded by kissing him and holding him tightly, but that summer she would never say the words he craved to hear.

A Pool of Thoughts

THE WORD around town was that the kid two streets over had jumped off the diving board the wrong way and broke his neck when he hit the water. He died, and the public swimming pool closed down shortly afterwards.

No one talked about the pool—or the boy— and we carried our thoughts (and fears) around with us like an overstuffed backpack for the rest of the summer.

Two summers later the pool reopened. The diving board had been removed, though.

I wish I could say I went back and learned to swim, but I couldn't bring myself to.

The Giants of Royal de Luxe

KHALILAH COULD HARDLY BELIEVE her eyes as she stared at the giants looming overhead, their arms, legs, and heads connected to giant wires moved by cranes and a team of puppeteers dressed in fine velvet. They took turns leaping onto a rope and jumping to the ground, each jump a step for the giant.

It was both amazing and terrifying.

As a giant turned its head, seemingly looking at her, Khalilah wondered if it might snap loose the strings binding it and walk toward her, crumbling the street in its wake.

If that happened, she decided she would befriend it.

The Woods

THEY CALLED the small undeveloped lot behind their grandmother's small house "the woods." During the daytime it was a place of wonder and adventure, a place where they could run and climb trees. Every once in a while they'd come across a garter snake and run back to the house, before slowly trudging back into the woods to resume whatever game they were playing.

At night, when the stars hung overhead like a star-flecked panorama, they gazed at the wall of darkness the woods had become.

Curiously, they wondered what things resided there that hadn't been there during the day.

Sara Bergman's Closet

THE PART I love most about this book is a tiny section that states Sara owned both real and fake Louis Vuitton bags. I wonder if anyone could tell.

In the movie *Dope*, one character noted most of the customers for his counterfeit bags were white women who could afford the real thing, but because of who they were, people assumed the bags to be real.

My cousin Marcus has a collection of rare sneakers he's never worn. If he ever put them on, I wonder whether people would look at his dark skin and believe they're real or not.

Ignominious

JAYSON HAD LEARNED the word in school. One of the week's ten vocabulary words. Mr. Wallace had told him if he used it three times, it would forever be his.

He started out by using it to describe his aunt's behavior, since she'd gotten drunk at his cousin's wedding reception and passed out.

Then he used it to describe the former mayor's arrest in an FBI prostitution ring sting.

By the time he had begun to enumerate the transgressions of his pastor at Mount Olive Church, everyone began to fear what Jayson's growing vocabulary would mean for them, as well.

Gibberish

JORDAN RETURNED from the woods speaking gibberish, but Malia wasn't alarmed. After all, she'd pretended to make up languages as a kid, too.

The next day she overheard him playing with his friends down the street.

They all spoke gibberish.

That evening Malia spoke with her wife about Jordan's behavior.

"I'll talk to him," she said, much to Malia's relief.

Minutes later, she reappeared, speaking gibberish.

"Lena, stop! You're scaring me!" is what Malia meant to say, but she could no longer recognize her own words, though somewhere in her mind, she was well aware of what she was saying.

Dark and Deep

THE MASSIVE POOL had been dyed pitch black, and as dusk arrived, the pool appeared even darker.

Anthony knew it was the same pool he swam in everyday, but it looked deeper somehow. He marveled at how color affected perception. He'd even heard that Alfred Hitchcock would dye a fine steak and potatoes dinner blue, just to see the reaction of his guests. This, however, felt different.

He leapt into the water, feeling as thought he was now hovering over an abyss.

Just then, something massive and smooth brushed beneath his feet.

He prayed that it was only the floor.

Soil

THOSE WHO HAD wings flew away. Those without wings remained, the purple soil gaining weight beneath their feet. Even the hastily constructed weapons shaped from the *Fucofina* trees felt like empty gestures, futile attempts to combat a technologically-advanced race that would stop at nothing to eradicate them.

In the distance they could hear the humming of drones, the snapping of branches far overhead, even the imagined whispers of an enemy they could actually see, possibly crawling through fallen leaves on scaled bellies.

But the drones would destroy them long before the enemy arrived, their remains trampled deep into the soil.

An Alien Concept

SANDRA FELT FAIRLY comfortable about the existence of extraterrestrials.

The sun was a star, and that star had eight planets (plus dwarf planets) around it. Only one of those eight could sustain carbon-based life using an atmospheric composition suitable for Earth life.

She could see the plethora of stars in the sky. Excluding those that were dead, their light still traveling through the universe, each of those stars contained planets with their own moons. Surely one of those many planets supported life of some sort.

We couldn't be the only life forms out there, she thought. *It's simple logic, right?*

One Big Sun

ONCE THE SCHOOL YEAR ENDED, Athena would travel to the various regions of the world she'd taught about during the fall and spring semesters of her literature classes at Ellison-Wright College. This was one of the annual indulgences she allowed herself.

One thing she noticed, however, after the citywide tours and the various museums, was that while there were tons of differences (languages, food, religions, and cultural behaviors), there was oftentimes a place where people would gather to watch the sun set against the western horizon.

These sunsets reminded her that all countries are a part of the same world.

The King-Size Ice Box

HE DRIFTED in and out of sleep, dazed, trying desperately to wrap his mind around the fact that she was no longer there. The sheets were cold, the pillow on the other side completely untouched.

Had he been too harsh?

He could still see the text messages on her phone, her pleas to a man he didn't know, her desires raging, but someone else was the kindling.

He tried to make it work, to give her another chance, but his trust had spoiled sour like month-old milk.

Still, nothing could ever prepare him for how cold his bed would become.

The Typewriter

HE BOUGHT a typewriter because he loved the sound of the keys clicking and the bell dinging at the end of each line. He'd always romanticized using one. When he finally bought one, though, he quickly learned that his typing skills were subpar and that he'd have to use a special eraser or Wite-Out to fix his errors. Plus, the weight of it was more than he'd bargained for, as it took two hands to carry it around—and he had to keep paper close at hand.

Content to just have it as a collectible, he returned to his laptop.

The Bulls

SHORTLY BEFORE EVERYTHING went to shit, Tommy traveled to Pamplona, Spain, to run with the bulls. It had been an item on his bucket list for quite some time, and he'd convinced himself it was time to stop putting it off.

He'd never ridden an adrenaline wave so strong, trying to outrun the heavy slapping of hooves against cobblestone, as people yelled in admiration and fear.

When the days of the pandemic wore on, he would remember the moment he ran so fast he couldn't feel his legs beneath him and know that he'd survived before and would survive again.

Floating

THEY FLOATED TOGETHER in the corner of the deep end of the pool, bobbing like apples, their taut bodies rubbing against each other, her stomach touching his, the smoothness of their legs intertwining beneath the water as they casually kicked.

They had promised that they wouldn't fall in love—the summer was littered with failed relationships—so they kept their feelings to themselves.

Neither wanted to drown in the emotions of the other, although they floated dangerously close to that. Instead, they continued to tread the water with their hands, their lips occasionally touching, but never really merging into one.

Memory Gaps

It's the "we were never gonna make it" part he keeps forgetting, lost in memories, moments, music blanketing them, sealing them, their bodies left to marinate between sheets that now rest at the bottom of a Goodwill bin.

He can still taste her, smell her, hear the sound of her voice and the sweet sighs of her sleep. Forever was a given. They thought they would never use their words as weapons, savagely slicing the other.

They didn't know their love had an expiration date.

No, he romanticizes their past because people block out those things that hurt them most.

Hero

THE CAPE WAS SO LONG he tripped over it, the blue polyester sticking to the soles of his Converses. "You know, all heroes don't wear capes," Pops told him.

The mask didn't fit well over his glasses, pressing the plastic frames into his face. "You know, all heroes don't wear masks," Mama told him.

His pigeon toes kept him from running fast. "You know, all heroes aren't fast," his brother told him.

He couldn't fly, lift a car, or turn invisible. "Being a hero is about caring for others and showing up," his family told him.

He could do that.

Wishing

SHE WORE COTTON SHORTS, white like Delta clouds, her brown legs peeking out from underneath and shining like melted chocolate, her Stan Smith Adidas white like lies with a kiss of mistletoe green on the heel, and her soft lips tasted like the sweet syrup of purple popsicles on a Saturday in July.

My mind was a wheel of fortune, my fingers crossed, hoping the right words would come (before I bankrupted) to freeze her in her tracks, lock this moment in our memories, a fossil where years later we could hold it and laugh at how silly we were.

The Candy Tax

BIG MAMA SAID, "Reach in my purse and pull out a five. Pick me up a pack of Camels from Joker's. And bring me back my change."

I put on the headphones to my Walkman and walked a block to the store on the corner.

Joker wasn't supposed to sell a pack of cigarettes to an eleven-year-old, but he knew how Big Mama did it.

He pulled down the pack without a word.

"And let me get two packs of Now & Laters. *Red.*"

Joe casually rung me up.

Big Mama never mentioned the candy.

She had nicotine. I had sugar.

Junior's Quick Stop

My wife doesn't trust gas station fried chicken, but, dammit, I do. In fact, I rank it among the best food in town, including those fancy chains, where they keep laying off the spices and seasonings every year.

I tell her that they *lovingly* marinate those breasts, before *gently* battering them and *patiently* submerging them into the hot oil.

She stops and contemplates this, then remembers we are talking about fried chicken.

"I just can't get my chicken from the same place I buy gas for my car," she finally says, never once considering the convenience of such a thing.

The Day My Sister Broke Ranks

IT HAD BEEN AN ESTABLISHED family rule from time immemorial that you stayed in your lane when it came to family cookouts. Big Mama made the sweet potato pies and the fried chicken, Papa took care of the catfish, Uncle Joe made the best cornbread, Aunt Marcy had the macaroni and cheese on lock, Aunt Nancy handled the greens, and Aunt Louise did the potato salad.

My sister, clearly a Generation Z'er, brought a second side of potato salad—with raisins in it.

No one corrected her, but they lovingly ignored her contribution, whispering "Bless her heart" beneath their breaths.

Ice Cream

On Saturdays, Uncle Dennis would pull his old blue Nissan into the backyard, and we'd gather around, full sponges, suds bubbling up between our fingers, washing in big circles like Daniel-san.

Earth, Wind & Fire blasted from the boom box on the back porch, the plug attached to an extension cord running past the screen door back into the house.

"Don't forget the tires!" he'd yell, while picking his hair.

He'd be taking his main squeeze out that night. We'd wash the car, and he'd pay us with ice cream money.

Looking back, I still feel that was a good deal.

Dreams of an MC

IN MY DREAM I am spitting. But not spitting like dropping bars. I am spitting *spit*, then blood, then teeth, wondering how long it'll take to get dentures.

When I try to speak, *to spit bars*, my mouth moves like it is stuck together with molasses. Eventually a sound emerges through my throat and vibrates past my lips. The sound wakes me.

Sitting on the edge of my bed, I rock back and forth to calm my nerves, reciting rhymes from an old notebook until I can re-establish verbal dexterity.

Then I fall asleep, words protecting me like a mouthguard.

When Niggas Turn Into Gods, Walls Come Tumbling...

AFTER FAT BELLY BELLA

MONK TOOK a deep puff and exhaled out his soul until the smoke filled the booth and he could no longer see the microphone. The words poured from a place beyond him, beyond the studio, beyond the protests, beyond the pain.

> I'm tired of being invisible
> In a nation supposedly indivisible

One day he could become a hashtag, but in this moment, behind that microphone, he was invincible, immortal. He was determined to craft his breath into songs, into art.

In the future, when people looked back at 2020, they would know that he was there, telling his own story.

Homecoming Dance at the
National Guard Armory

SHE KNEW he couldn't palm a basketball, but she allowed him to palm her ass, which she figured was much softer (more like a fresh bag of carnival cotton candy) than the hardwood leather he had trouble handling on the court.

She carried him just off the beat, like a Questlove snare hanging over a measure. She didn't mind his hand, though. At least *that* part of her wasn't stuffed with tissue.

His breath smelled like hot Vienna sausages and peppermint, and he kept trying to sing Keith Sweat's part on "Make It Last Forever," always just a little off-key.

Water

Big Mama's funeral was on the twelfth day of summer. We dressed in black, sucking in the blasts of the sun's breath, our bodies crying water from every pore.

The graveside service had gone on too long, our fans unable to keep up with the suffocating heat. Sweat ran into our eyes, stinging our tears, and we fought the urge to think about the repast, where an air conditioner awaited us.

The pastor, seemingly oblivious, droned on, though, until eventually Big Arthur passed out, his knees locked. He fell like a great oak struck by lightning.

The benediction quickly followed.

Stuck

I HATED when my parents took us to visit Aunt Lulabelle. As restless kids, we had nothing to do but stare at her faded yellow and tan wallpaper, anthropomorphizing the 70's-styled repetitive flower patterns.

Sometimes we'd have to go sit in her living room—but we couldn't play in there, for fear of knocking over a crystal vase or something.

The air conditioner in the kitchen didn't blow in there very well, so my sister and I would sit, the backs of our thighs stuck to the plastic on the couch, wanting to leave, but too afraid to stand.

Uncle Red's Unorthodox Advice
For Approaching Fine Women

UNCLE RED's cure for Little Carlos being nervous around girls:

"There're two types of people: those who wipe and look and those who wipe and don't. If you're in the first group, your eyes are on *the prize*. What does that say about you?

"Now the second group is using 'the force' to feel things. Those are the ones who start getting that itch later. What does that say about them?

"It's human to do either of the two—and every human's got to make a choice.

"Fine women are human, too. They're not exempt from this. *Catch my drift?*"

Nike's SNKRS App Won't Let Me Be Great

I JUST CAN'T CATCH a break.

I'm up early on Saturday mornings—sometimes Thursdays and the occasion Tuesday or Friday—to cop a pair of kicks I've been eyeing for over six months. A limited drop, another pair of J's I probably don't even need, all to be dope, get the nod from heads in the know, round out the collection, stunt on these motherfuckers (because during a pandemic what else is there to do?).

Just one pair.

I'm not even trying to resell.

I will definitely cop and rock.

But this damn app won't even let me be great.

Soundtrack

THEY'D PARTED ways over twenty years ago—
had even built their own families—but they remained tethered to each other through a single
song, their nineteen-year-old selves locked eter-
nally within those four minutes of Johnny Gill
singing "I'm Still Waiting," beckoning them
back to a place in time where the song once
played on repeat in his sophomore dorm room,
scented candles flickering against the autumn
darkness, while they did their best to make love
to every square inch of each other's being.

Although their relationship had come to an
end, the song refused to let either of them go.

A Hair Story

"WHEN YOU GON' cut that boy's hair?" Uncle Morgan asked.

"He can grow it as long as he wants. It's *his* hair," my mother responded.

"You ain't worried about him lookin' like a girl?"

My mother paused a bit too long before answering, "Nope."

I sat between Grandma's thighs on the house steps, her hands smelling like coco butter and coconut oil, as she braided my hair, which was now down to my shoulders.

"Samson's strength was in his hair," Grandma reminded me.

"But do I look like a girl?" I asked.

"You look just like one of God's children."

"Hot Sauce In My Bag" Swag

"You really carry hot sauce in your bag?" Nick asked Aniyah.

"Yep."

"Is it a Beyoncé thing?"

"Nope. I've always carried hot sauce in my bag."

"And you use it?" Nick asked, realizing the stupidity of his question. "Around *white people*, I mean?"

"Why not? If the food needs a hit, I give it a hit. I don't care who's around."

"I don't know if I could do that, stereotypes about us and all."

"Well, you have to do you, just like I have to do me."

Nick looked at his catfish plate and grimaced. "Can I borrow some?"

"Nope."

Portmanteau

HE COULDN'T TELL if it was a compliment or a derision. She had said it matter-of-factly, as if he should have known what it meant. He prided himself on knowing these things, things that were in the vernacular of popular culture. Through context clues, he had figured out what "being on *fleek*" was. He had even managed to grasp "turnt up" fairly quickly. See, it was a matter of breaking down the words individually and then putting their meanings together collectively. This word, however, was different. Was it sexual? Was it the opposite? He'd never been called a *fuckboy* before.

The Writer

AFTER YEARS of waking up to rejections from editors, agents and publishers, Gary put all of his unpublished stories, novellas, and novels into a folder marked "Do Not Resuscitate" on his desktop. *Sometimes the things you love just don't love you back,* he thought.

He looked at a few cameras, some DSLRs and even a few fix-lensed mirrorless ones, unsure if photography could scratch the same itch.

He then taught himself to play the guitar, hoping music would do it.

But in the end, he returned to his original passion: writing.

He realized the world's affirmation was not a requirement.

Talons (Redux)

SHE PINNED him to her bed, her fingers like claws, her nails pinching his flesh. He was so hungry for her that he didn't feel the blood dripping down his arms or notice the large wings emerging from her back and stretching wide over the bed, blocking out the street light pouring through her parted window blinds.

His eyes closed, he enjoyed the feeling of her body moving above him, surprised by how committed she was to this character.

Then she squawked in climax, and he opened his eyes, just in time to see his flesh dangling from her beak.

Open Mic

LOVE JONES HAD MADE Akeem into a horrible poet. In lieu of studying real poets, he wrote second-rate poems, all designed to woo some woman in the audience.

He also looked the part: wearing a pair of prescription-less glasses and carrying a Moleskine notebook around with him.

The other poets weren't impressed, though, nicknaming him "the poet who didn't know it," quietly laughing as he read, and snapping their fingers in jest when he finished.

They had no idea he was studying *them* and reading *their* favorite poets and that one day he'd actually be even better than they were.

The Sneaker Grail

AFTER YEARS OF SEARCHING, Wallace had finally found them.

He admired their golden color, surprised at how heavy they were. He was briefly reminded of his first pair of Air Jordan 1 OG highs, smelling the insides of the shoes, fresh out the box. He'd come a long way since then, both literally and figuratively, as he stood in the small shoe shop in Rome.

Wallace knew they were legit. Only two people had ever worn them.

He, however, planned to never wear the Talaria of Mercury. Still, he couldn't help wondering what Michael Jordan would have done in them.

Washington Square Park

THE LITTLE BOY sat down across from Ivan Chernyshevsky and moved a pawn.

"Why you come here and do this to yourself? You never win," Ivan said, shaking his head slowly.

"My father used to come here to play—before he died," the little boy responded.

"Really? What was his name?"

"Charles Lewis."

Ivan nodded. "And you? Your name?"

"Tobin."

Ivan rubbed his hands together to warm them, then rubbed his thick beard. "Well, Tobin, first thing to learn is white goes first. That means I go first. Then *you* play."

Tobin nodded.

"Don't worry, kid. I will teach you."

Pillows

WHENEVER I HAD nightmares when I was growing up, my mother would pretend to throw away my pillow, claiming the bad dreams came from inside of it. She claimed to buy another pillow, and I'd use that one until, inevitably, I had another nightmare.

Years after I had served three tours in the army did it occur to me that my mother did not buy me all those pillows. She was working two jobs to feed five kids.

She just needed for me to believe I could fight my fears until I was actually old enough to really do it.

The Daily Public Library

BY THE TIME I reached the library and put my bike on the rack, my t-shirt was stuck to my back with sweat. But the library would be cool inside.

The head librarian, Mrs. Patterson, nodded to me. "You doing the Pizza Hut BOOK IT! Program this summer?"

"Yes, ma'am," I responded, fluffing my shirt to let in some of the air conditioning.

I walked the aisles, taking my time, pulling down mysteries and science fiction, horror and humor, drying off.

Next week I'd have enough for a personal pan, but for me, it was about more than the pizza.

Dreams of Barack's Jalopy

FOR A WEEK, Marlon dreamed Barack Obama was trying to sell him a magical used car. It was the car Barack had been driving when he started dating Michelle.

There wasn't much to it: an ugly yellow Datsun with a rusted-out hole in the floorboard that allowed you to see the street beneath the car.

"It's done wonders for me," Barack said.

Marlon studied the jalopy, trying his best to sense magic in it. "I don't know," he finally said.

"Well, think on it," Barack responded.

In his dreams, Marlon never bought the car, but wondered if he should have.

There Was An Old Lady...

THIS IS how the story goes: The was an old lady who lived in an Air Jordan 1 OG High Travis Scott/ Fragment collab sneaker. She had so many children wandering about and getting into shit that people threaten to call protective services on her—more than once. So that broth/bread thing with the switch was out.

Then a *hypebeast* made her an offer on the sneaker.

She quickly traded that leather, rubber, and glue for a house with a backyard.

Now I hear her kids are on the honor roll and that she's happier than she's ever been.

The Love Letter

HE'D PATIENTLY WRITE each line of the letter in his best cursive, his hand dancing with the page, caressing his notions of her, some words floating above the linen paper, all melodies born of his fantasy of what they could be.

One page was not enough; he wanted her to spend hours inside his poetry, so he mined his mind of the verbal jewels that would ultimately pale in comparison to the simple beauty of her smile.

Afterwards, he'd spray his cologne once into the air and allow the letter to catch the precipitation, before sealing it with a kiss.

The Reenactor

THE REENACTOR MOVED about the colonial community, as one tourist gazed hungrily, offering his unsolicited commentary.

"Hey, slave, you forgot to pick up that piece of trash over there."

Nathan blinked hard, but stayed in character. His character was free.

"If you were my slave, I'd beat the black off your ass for disobedience," the heavyset white guy added, his face glowing red.

Nathan had once discovered an old cat o' nine tails in a shack on the plantation. Appalled, he took it and started carrying it with him beneath his shirt.

The tourist had no idea what hit him.

Blackfishing

THE WHITE GIRLS began tanning their skin and braiding their hair, using lipstick to thicken the appearance of their lips, doing squats, rocking Jordans, and practicing their twerking. They knew the lyrics to the most popular rap songs and openly pined over Black athletes and actors. They swore it wasn't a phase they were going through.

As they masqueraded on into the night of the Negro Solstice[1], they awoke the following morning to find they were unable to undo their hair and that their tans had darkened considerably.

Terrified, they told anyone who would listen that they weren't *really* Black.

---

1. *December 21, 2020, was comedically designated the Negro Solstice by Twitter users, claiming Black people gained superpowers during the eclipse. Note: the author of this story is still waiting for his powers to kick in.*

Saxophonic Dreams

HE COULD HEAR the melodies in his dreams, his fingers fluttering against the mattress of his bed. His mind raced to keep up with the notes, his tongue darting against the backs of his teeth.

His saxophone rested in a case on the dresser next to the bed, its insides cool, waiting, wanting…

He sometimes walked around with a reed between his lips, the way a farmer might hold a blade of grass, occasionally moistening it, always anticipating the music.

At night when they joined up with the quartet, he and his saxophone would recreate their dreams with euphonic bliss.

True Crime

SHE COULDN'T EXPLAIN her attraction to true crime podcasts. Maybe it was the mystery of it all, the chance to solve puzzles (or to see how they were solved). Maybe it was because she enjoyed a good story (always had). Most of the podcasts used a story structure that was equally, if not more, interesting than the syndicated scripted television shows she watched repeatedly.

At the heart of each episode, though, was a crime—usually a murder. Often times the victim was a young woman, like herself.

Maybe the podcasts were a way of facing her fears.

She hoped not.

The Wolfgang Jefferson Volume

DEEPLY EMBEDDED in the library's stacks is a bound leather journal containing the handwritten escapades of Wolfgang Jefferson, who escaped bondage in 1858 by flying back to Africa. Legend has it that as Wolfgang hovered over what is now Lagos, he saw that white men had infiltrated his home country. He eventually settled on Haiti, but his progeny gradually found its way back to American soil, the journal passed down from generation to generation, until it was acquired by an affluent collector and donated to the Ralph Ellison Library at Ellison-Wright College in Atlanta, a place now considered its home.

The Book Club

CYNTHIA STARTED the novel four times before finally deciding to put it down. The novel had been *her* choice for the book club, a change from the usual romances and mysteries she felt were not serious enough for her tastes.

She'd heard about the novel on NPR, and the group had accepted the recommendation without challenge.

When they finally met to discuss the book, everyone had read and enjoyed the book, everyone except Cynthia, who couldn't bring herself to finish it.

As the club continued to read more challenging books, Cynthia had to leave the club to find another one.

Lonely

HE WAS FROM A BIG CITY, where people were always on a quest to find the latest and greatest of anything, but she was from a town so small the local DJ, who'd had a stroke and his voice slurred heavily, held down the number one radio show in the county, purely based on the respect afforded him by his longtime listeners.

She knew deep down that they saw the world too differently, but loneliness was a beast that forced her to look past who she was in order to become someone whose main attribute was that she wasn't lonely.

Searching for Water Where It Never Rains

THEY FANCIED themselves the up-and-coming moguls, the ones who would take over the city, the recent graduates who populated the bars, the gentlemen puffing Cohibas, the ladies holding court on the finest of French wines, preparing their pretentious palates for a wealth that awaited them, like seven-figure gated estates, where their neighbors were top draft picks or music producers who were no strangers to the Billboard charts, but amid this atmosphere of affluence, they complained not of the money, but of their lack of significant others, the people for whom they'd left just enough space for their mahogany trophy cases.

The Yearbook

HOURS after the school year ended, Kenyatta lay on his bed, the sounds of Troop's "Spread My Wings" in the background, reading the beautifully rendered inscription left in his yearbook by Deja Brooks.

He'd, over the course of several months, worked up the nerve to speak to her each day, often times trying to catch her in the main hallway between third and fourth periods, as if by accident. Now she'd written him five neat lines of cursive and used the closing "love" to top it off.

He'd cherish it, knowing he'd never have the courage to go any farther.

Wolfgang V's Cabinet of Curiosities

WHEN WOLFGANG V DIED, he left behind an unusual cabinet of curiosities: a blanket made from the skin of a manatee that had died of natural causes; the tusk of a walrus that had been transformed into some sort of flute; a Bible Wolfgang Sr. had handed down; a rusted chattel chain, also handed down from Wolfgang Sr.; a blunt axe, alleged to have been a weapon used during an insurrection; and an array of photographs and first edition leather-bound books that had been acquired over the course of a lifetime of international travel. Ellison-Wright College acquired these objects, too.

The Seasons Know Exactly When to Change

HE WANTED her to love him at least one day past the expiration date of their relationship. Not that it would have made a difference. He now understood that he couldn't will her to feel anything she wasn't already inclined to feel. There was someone else. Someone better.

He didn't want to be one of those men wallowing in self-pity, wondering if his calloused hands and work boots could ever measure up to her new beau's metrosexuality.

People don't belong to other people, and she was never his. Their time was intertwined, finite, like seasons that were destined to change.

The Man of Her Dreams

HE'D NEVER DONE anything untoward to her, in word or deed, so she found her dreams to be a bit of a mystery.

He was a gentleman, a patient soul, always concerned with her feelings, cherishing her opinions—but as she slept, that same man, the man she believed she loved, haunted her in her dreams, chasing her with unusual weapons, like harpoons, bear traps, handheld gardening cultivators, steel meat tenderizers, and even a molten pot of grits.

She knew he would never understand her "Dear John" letter (nor would she), but she knew she could never stay with him.

Poultry

CARLOS and his daughter sat at one of the rustic picnic tables sparsely scattered around Bluebird Gap Farm. Trying to create an impromptu lunch picnic for her, since she was on spring break from middle school, he picked up chicken tenders and fries for them.

As they quietly ate, a free-roaming peacock sauntered over to their table (perhaps hoping for a piece of bread that wasn't there) and stood there staring at them.

"Dad, don't feed him anything. That would be, like, cannibalism."

Carlos considered this and quietly packed up their food, easing past the peacock back to their car.

The Official Lyrics to "Gobbledygook"

[1]*Iguana tennis shoe/she commode jump
the fire squad/dingaling game
strong/Swayze stucko/fuckboy ge-
nius/mellow mojo no ho so fo' real
doe/dream like Tetris/Abbey
crazy/but I love you like an upside
down rainbow/roundhouse town-
house/micromania/she insanity
like wallpaper/Chimamanda
daze/Vasoline gasoline/but I love
you like an upside down rain-
bow/Lennon lyric/spinal
saltine/we surrender to the fog/fat
boy dangerous wish/like
sausage/but I love you like an upside down rainbow, an upside
down rainbow*

1. *These are the original song lyrics as written in Oblongata Jones's
notebook, circa 2019.*

All Deliberate Speed

FOR DAD

TERRELL LISTENED to his father talk about *Brown v. Board of Education, Topeka, Kansas*, thinking it odd that the subject had even come up.

"The opinion for that case came down when I was starting high school in 1954. The school district in my hometown had finally integrated by the time I finished college in 1969.

"Justice Black had warned the Court that places like Mississippi would take their time. And he was right."

Terrell listened, unable to imagine what that must have been like, but as he stared at his father's pinched lips and furrowed brow, he could understand.

We Been Livin' Through Your Internet

TONYA DIDN'T KNOW what to think when her sixteen-year-old son, Lavell, revealed to her that the only thing he wanted for Christmas was to not be a hashtag.

He had been watching a television show centered around the Black Lives Matter movement, and the final episode had concluded with a list of hashtags for unarmed Black men and women who were killed by police officers. The black background had turned white from the overlapping text of the hashtags.

Secretly, Tonya wanted the same thing, even though it was the kind of thing they shouldn't have ever had to wish for.

Diaries of the Deceased

EVELYN'S JAW dropped as she watched the bid on the used diary quickly approach $500. While she often journaled, it was only recently that she'd become interested in the used journals of other people.

This particular journal had belonged to an award-winning poet who had lost her battle with breast cancer five years earlier. The journal was an Italian leather-bound A5 with ruled cream-colored pages. Nearly every page had been written on, and several early drafts of the poet's published poems appeared therein.

Evelyn would ultimately lose the auction, but, in that prior heady moment, she'd found herself genuinely inspired.

Metal Clouds

HE CHANGED the clothes he wore and the music he listened to, hoping to erase as many memories of her as he could, but there were days when the wind blew a certain way or the rain seemed to cry from the sky and he was left standing in a moment where love kissed his vulnerable spots and he could only mutter her name.

But she'd moved on, as he struggled to do.

Sometimes he hated himself for being so weak, for being unable to recollect those moments when she'd bristled at his touch, for not letting her go sooner.

Talent

ON HIS DEATH BED, Charlie Brogan revealed to his children and grandchildren a secret he'd carried around with him his entire life: he could eat metal.

They looked at him confused, unsure of what to think.

"I had a real life super power," he managed, his breath sputtering.

"Did you ever use it?" the youngest grandchild asked.

"I never could figure out what to do with it."

Suddenly, he thought to cough up a silver dollar, which he handed to the child, who took it, smiling.

Charlie'd found a use for his talent, and with that, he could now rest.

Bearded

Nala had politely asked Shemeik several times to shave his beard, but he had refused. He prided himself on being a great lover—of this, Nala agreed completely—but the beard sometimes got in the way. It also had the tendency to collect fluids, which, in and of itself, was quite embarrassing.

He didn't seem to mind, but Nala had trouble looking at him, his thick, shiny beard glistening with its glazed coating, as he tried, unsuccessfully, to kiss her mouth afterwards.

One night as he slept, she shaved him.

He liked it, which, unbeknownst to him, saved their relationship.

The Monster in the Woods

ANZEL COLLIER HAD BEEN the first kid to see the monster in the woods. He described the beast as an ape-like man moving rapidly through the thicket. Other kids would later report seeing something similar, so the sheriff's department had no choice but to investigate it.

After staking out the woods for a day, they finally saw this so-called monster emerge from behind a large clump of trees.

"Hey!" shouted the sheriff. "Stop!"

The monster froze in its tracks.

"Dammit, Angus! If you're gonna cheat, get a hotel room—and try shaving once in a while. You're scaring the kids!"

Glitter

IN THE END, it was the glitter that saved her, those fine flecks of magenta plastic and aluminum that she carried around in her backpack for various art projects. That bottle was the only weapon she had, so when the creepy man from the van across the street from the school grabbed her arm, she flung it directly into his bug eyes and took off running.

Unable to drive, he stomped and cursed while leaning against his van, and those minutes of incapacitating irritation were all it took for students to alert officers, who could then take him into custody.

The 100-Word Story

FOR DR. EUGENE REDMOND, CREATOR OF THE KWANSABA

SHE DARED him to write a 100-word story using no word longer than seven letters, much like the Black poetic form that uses the same rule, and he said that he'd try.

So he sat down at his laptop and began to write a very unusual story, a meta tale of a Black man who is writing a story using only words that are seven letters or fewer. The man in that story is also writing a story about a man, who is writing a story about another man, who happens to be writing the story that you are reading.

The Castle

IT WAS the final thing on her bucket list: visiting the Neuschwanstein Castle in Bavaria, Germany. After years of her father taking her to Disneyland, he'd revealed to her the source of the Magic Kingdom's inspiration, and in the years that followed, she planned how she would one day visit the castle.

Now that the day had arrived and she stood before it, her eyes filled with tears, but not the tears that accompany the fulfillment of a dream; they were tears from the realization that this was the only time in her life that she would behold this beauty.

Wolfgang VII at Ellison-Wright College

ON SATURDAY MORNINGS, Wolfgang VII would walk from his dorm across campus to the Ralph Ellison Library to see his grandfather's collection, as well as the other artifacts the college had secured in the past 100 years that had belonged to his ancestors. He might've attended Ellison-Wright College anyway, but the fact that it housed his legacy made his enrollment there a no-brainer.

Every once in a while, he thought about taking back those items and fleeing the campus, but he knew it was better for those things to be protected and cherished, available for all to appreciate and admire.

Wings

ON SATURDAY MORNING, Bria woke up to find that she'd grown a rather large set of wings on her back. As she stood before the mirror on her closet door, she allowed the wings to unfurl to their full length. She didn't know if she could fly, but she felt that she could, if given the chance to try.

The wings provided a slight hump to her back, which she planned to conceal with hooded sweatshirts. In the summer she could use a backpack.

She didn't complain, though. It could've always been worse. She could have woken up a beetle.

On "Home Alone"

As my sister and I watched *Home Alone* for the umpteenth time, she casually offered, "If I were Kevin, I would have let those burglars in and told them that they could steal whatever they wanted, as long as they didn't touch my stuff."

Astonished, I looked at her, trying to make sense of her comment. Then finally I asked, "Why?"

She smiled, as if it were obvious. "They left that little boy behind and were a few hours along into their flight to France before they even realized it."

I allowed her rationale to wash over me— and agreed.

Library Dreams

HE SLEPT with a volume of Jorge Luis Borges's collected short stories beneath his pillow and swore that it influenced his dreams. He would wander through labyrinthine libraries, walls of books guiding him to some unknown destination. Occasionally he'd see cats or sheep that moved like humans, but that was normally in the Murakami wing. Some nights he would fly up to the highest shelves, while other nights he would open books and dive into their liquid pages. In the end, he'd find his way back to his bed, where he would awake the following morning, still exhausted but satisfied.

The Last Novel

MALCOLM HALEY, after a full and rewarding career as a novelist, decided the last book he wrote would be self-published. He'd published the same way (traditionally) for decades, and while he was able to scrape out a living, he always felt like the final versions were in many ways compromised. This new book, however, found him at his most vulnerable. Not particularly concerned with sales, he did little in the way of monitoring its sales. Even more, he had trouble digesting the idea that his book would win an Alexandre Literary Award, the first ever in his entire career.

Black Water

SHE HAD nightmares of black water trickling from the hotel faucet, shooting out from the shower head, swirling around the commode, and even dripping from her toothbrush. It was always black water, and the water had always come from above, a tank on a higher floor, or perhaps the roof, containing the body of a woman thought to have disappeared.

In her dreams the water would pool at her feet, before rising slowly up her calves to her thighs and hips, forming a black liquid curtain around her body. Then it would pull her until she slid down the drain.

The Mystery of Death

IN THE DAYS leading up to Parker Madison's death, he had visited several mediums along the downtown tourist strip. He wasn't attempting to contact a deceased family member. No. His goal was much simpler: he wanted to determine what, if anything, happened after a person died.

Perhaps he was a bit too skeptical to buy into anything the mediums told him, but he'd always been skeptical, even as a kid when he used to sit, twiddling his thumbs in mass.

Now, he realized the truth came only when you found out things for yourself.

And that's exactly what he did.

Famous Writers

HE LONGED to be one of those writers reviewers referenced when blurbing other authors. ("It's like [famous writer/*him*] was writing alongside [famous writer/*someone else*]. That was the hallmark of fame, not book sales. Your name had to become enmeshed in the culture. The idea of you had to transcend who you really were. That was the only success worth striving for.

Moreover, he cherished the idea of "esque" being added to his surname, thereby transcending literature itself. People would say the situation in which they found themselves was *XXX-esque* and he'd smile from a distance, as Kafka might've.

Monthly Chips

At 4'10" and with a young appearance, Janice was used to being carded whenever she entered the casino. After making her way past security, she'd head straight for the poker room to buy in.

Texas Hold 'Em was her game of choice. While dice had better odds, this was the one game where the casino didn't factor into wins or losses. She simply had to play the seven people at her table.

Legs swinging above the floor, Janice had learned that men often underestimated women, especially small ones. This table was no different.

She'd easily make her rent money.

Rodents

By the third date, they decided it was time to put all of the cards on the table, warts and all.

"I have a capybara living in my house," she said,

"A what?"

"A capybara."

"And what is a *capybara*?" he asked.

"It's the largest rodent in the world…"

She continued talking, but all he could see was her lips moving. Having grown up in an apartment in New York City, he could recollect times when the rat trap would go off and he could hear the rat dragging the trap.

"Yeah," he finally said. "This isn't going to work."

The Legendary Battle of Two Emcees

LEGEND HAS it that Oblongata Jones and Marz Banx faced off in the stairwell of the south tower of Wilder Projects back in 1998. Deez Nutz Even was the beatboxer, and before an astonished crowd of old heads and teenagers, the two emcees traded bars in the tradition of the legendary hip hop greats.

There's a rumor that someone recorded the battle on a mini-cassette tape, but it has yet to surface. Only the lucky souls in attendance can attest to the magic that took place there, words like liquid swords slicing the hungry air and transcending the art form.

An Origin Story

Tinesha quietly moved about her house, carefully carving a space for herself amid her seven brothers and sisters. The cacophony of raised voices, each one competing with the next for auditory supremacy, made it difficult for her to make out any individual words or phrases. She found a corner, usually unoccupied, save a haphazardly positioned jacket or backpack falling off a folding chair. She took a seat, her body so slight it barely disturbed the things around her.

She wanted to tell her parents and her siblings that she had gained a superpower during the eclipse—invisibility—but she didn't.

Dictionary Examples

Kakorrhaphiophobia (NOUN) - the fear of failure

Example: Vernon often daydreamed about leaving the small town of Daily, Mississippi, and going to New York City, where he could hopefully one day build an acting career on Broadway, but his kakorrhaphiophobia prevented him from actually doing anything to achieve his goal.

Schadenfreude (noun) - pleasure derived from knowing that someone has failed

Example: Vernon's sister, Vanessa, decided after she graduated from high school she would move to New York City to pursue an acting career, and while Vernon tried to be happy for her, he was filled with an overwhelming sense of schadenfreude.

A Math Problem

ALVIN HAD ONE HEART, and he gave it to Cherri. Cherri held on to it for three months before she decided to strap a piece of C4 to it and blow it up into 1,000 pieces, before walking away.

A year later, Alvin meets Jane. They hit it off tremendously, and Jane begins talking about giving her heart to Alvin. Alvin, still, shell shocked from his experience with Cherri, is suddenly uncomfortable—because his heart was blown into 1,000 pieces.

Questions: How long will it take Alvin to collect those 1,000 pieces, and could he give them to someone else?

The Miniaturist

THE WORLD he created was a tiny one, chairs smaller than nickels. The trick was to build each piece in proportion to the other. The table couldn't be too high for the chairs; the microwave had to be a perfect complement to the stove in both size and color. Each piece had to be perfect.

His daughter once asked him why he was so diligent with the miniatures that he built. Even though he didn't have a solid answer for her, he realized that there was something peaceful about being able to control things in a world that felt random.

Big Mama's Recipe

THE TURMOIL within the family had always been there, brothers and sisters bickering and cousins ignoring each other, but Big Mama thought she could bring everyone together while she lay in her deathbed.

They all agreed to put aside their grievances for the greater good of the family, and Big Mama transitioned peacefully.

After her funeral and repast, however, the family members arrived home to find the canister containing all of Big Mama's recipes had been stolen, reigniting the family war all over again.

Eventually, a private investigator was hired to taste every sweet potato pie from Mississippi to Mississauga.

Brunswick

THE RUGGED WHITE men hung over the edges of their pickup, like sailors on some colonial vessel, the Gadsen flag flying in the breeze as it had, for different reasons, hundreds of years ago, while they thundered down the road, adrenaline pulsing through their veins, their brains already working to create the myth on which their actions would stand. The Black boy may as well have been Moby Dick, though his jaws held no bones, for these men had already decided they would hunt him until they caught him, thinking their ocean would one day be safe to navigate again.

Hip Hop Is Dead, Long Live Hip Hop

"WHAT COMES AFTER HIP HOP?" my nephew once asked me.

He fancied me a scholar of sorts, had listened intently when I talked about the four elements (DJ, B-Boy/Girl, Emcee, and Graffiti Artist)—plus knowledge and beatboxing—and how other previous Black artistic movements had reflected similar elements. He had heard the old heads whispering (sometimes shouting) that Hip Hop was dead. But how could it be when it affected everything around us: politics, religion, business? Hip Hop has a way of constantly reinventing itself, always poised to remix its past. I didn't know what to tell him.

"Nothing."

Adrienne Dorine

CORLISS HAD COMPLETELY FORGOTTEN that she still had the doll. It had been buried in a box of things that she had carried from home to college to grad school to her first apartment to her second apartment and then to the home she shared with her husband and children. Little Sandy had been tunneling through boxes for fun and came across the Cabbage Patch doll.

"Mom, look what I found," she said, holding it up.

Corliss hadn't expected the feelings of nostalgia to rush over her. Suddenly, she was seven-years-old again, reliving the joy of Christmas morning in 1983.

Nothing

SEINFELD DID A SHOW ABOUT NOTHING.

Wale did an album about nothing.

So Raphael decided to write a novel about nothing.

Of course, his nothing was nothing like The Nothing from Ende's *The Neverending Story* (which, as it turned out, was actually something). No, his book would be aimless and meandering, but not in the way of a person wondering the streets of a city like Joyce's *Ulysses* or Cole's *Open City*. But the book couldn't be gibberish like a random Beatles lyric or even a song by Oblongata Jones.

He would just write whatever, if that were even possible.

The Art of the Steal

In the years before he was widely recognized as one of the greatest artists of his generation, he'd been a student at Ellison-Wright College, where, during the mid-sixties, while navigating the stacks of the library, he'd come across a collection of art books, most of which had never been checked out, though they'd been on the shelves for years.

One day he appeared in a natty trench coat and slid a single volume underneath it. It wasn't his original intention to steal the book, but by the time he'd graduated, he'd liberated the entire collection to his off campus apartment.

.Paak

IN MY DREAMS, I hear my dad's percussive steps in the next room, darkness descending upon my mother. Her breathing and heartbeat are percussion.

Years later, the phone ringing during class telling me my mom's in jail, too—all percussion. Hands sorting cannabis, leaves rustling, percussion. Homeless, hands on the steering wheel, baby in the backseat, I hear percussion.

Yes, Lawd. I hear the rhythms, feel them creeping up my arms and into my fingertips. I can no longer contain the music, and the moment my hands envelop the drum sticks, I am prepared to blast off into outer space.

The Price Is Right

WHEN OBLONGATA JONES WAS THREE, he sat on the carpet of Ms. Tremont's home daycare watching *The Price Is Right*, his LEGO blocks spread across the floor in front of him. He enjoyed the show, though he could only vaguely understand the games. He knew there were numbers and that some were good, while others were bad. The thing that stood out the most, though, was the music. His mind would wander as he listened and built tiny castles, not realizing that when he became a celebrity many years later, he'd begin his career by sampling the show's musical cues.

The Strange Animal Society

THE GROUP GRUNTED in amusement when Norma rose to her feet in her usual apodictic way and declared the gharial should be their animal of the year. Sure, there was some fascination with the reptile's appearance, particularly the boss at the tip of the male's snout, but not enough for the members to be thoroughly enraptured.

The shoebill stork and the atretochoana eiselti (better known as the "penis snake") were met with similar apathy.

After great debate, and much to Norma's chagrin, the group ultimately selected the homo sapien as its "Strange Animal of the Year," given its perplexing strangeness.

The Worst Graduation Speech Ever

So as I close, graduating class of 2022, I want you to acknowledge your dreams.

But when your dreams take control of you, they can turn you out. Have you on the stroll, on your knees in an alley or flat on you back with your heels up in the air or handcuffed up against a wall with a feather duster. Your dreams, taking *long* strokes on your soul, can have you looking in the mirror, scared, while standing in the back of a truck stop in Wisconsin.

Dreams are a dangerous thing, if you can't control them.

Thank you.

An Advertisement for Pet Toys

AS EVERY PROXIMALIAN KNOWS, humans can make horrible pets. Sure, they only need food and water and occasional light—maybe some clothing—but they're moody and largely violent. They are more entitled than all other earthling animals.

But we have a solution! Introducing Miniscreens™, the most effective way to keep your humans occupied. These devices are loaded with content of them doing humorous or horrific things to each other—and they love it!

For a limited time, we are offering you every tenth device free of charge. Act now before we run out! You, too, can have a happy human!

Bricks, Pt. 1

FIVE MINUTES before Professor Samuel's Intro to Sociology class started, all of the students' phones suddenly powered off, completely bricking.

"Professor Samuel, we have to cancel class!" one student yelled.

"My phone doesn't work, and I need to go get this checked on ASAP!"

"What if my parents try to call me while I'm in class?"

Professor Samuel cleared his throat. "When I was in college, we didn't even have mobile phones, let alone smartphones."

They looked at him quizzically, the room so quiet you could hear a mouse urinate on cotton.

Knowing they wouldn't stay, he reluctantly dismissed class.

Bricks, Pt. 2

Professor Samuel nearly tripped over several students standing in the parking lot looking into the air. The thing hovered in the sky above the school. *So much for the phones*, he thought, as his stomach sunk.

Suddenly, one of the students rose into the air, his movement so startling that those around him stood back. By the time anyone reached for the student's dangling leg, he was halfway to the floating object.

Once the student reached the object, both he and the object disappeared.

Everyone stood frozen, mouths agape.

Professor Samuel wasn't sure, but the student looked like Wolfgang VII.

Dreams of Home

I PEDALED my old bicycle to the end of my hometown street, and as I waited at the stop sign of Sixth Street, which intersected perpendicularly with Main Street, I had no idea of where I was going.

I thought of my address, a place in Hampton, Virginia, and while I carried the maps of various cities in my head (Atlanta, New York City, West Point, Jackson [Tennessee], and Hampton), they had merged into a single place.

A driver pulled up beside me and asked if I needed help.

Confused and afraid, I said, "I'm just trying to get home."

Change
_____

IN HIS ATTEMPTS TO explain the new direction of his life to his parents, he employed this metaphor:

All of my life, I have been a Jordan head, rocking the latest heat, damn near a hypebeast with a closet full of 1s, 3s, 4s, and 11s. And that was cool—for a while.

Now I'm sensing I need a change, a chance to step away from the hype and truly be myself. It's time for me to rock my Air Max 1s.

Of course his parents didn't understand this, but they understood what it was like to long for change.

The Mountain

DEJA RAE STOOD at the foot of the mountain, watching the sunlight pierce through it. The mountain was now the largest recorded in the history of the world, and it still managed to grow a little each year.

Some of the people in her village referred to it as a giant bubble. Her great-grandmother once said, "It's not much to look at, but at least it's here, where it can't cause any more problems."

Deja didn't know what her great-grandmother meant, but she couldn't imagine anything about the mountain being bad.

She just wanted to admire all of the plastic.

The Reviews

EVEN THOUGH, for the most part, the book was reviewed favorably, the critics seemed to home in on the chapters involving the descendants of the enslaved man who had flown to Africa, then on to Haiti. They couldn't make sense of the stories, although they sensed there was a connection between them. One critic even opined the author had run out of ideas when he wrote that the descendant of said enslaved man was abducted by aliens in the parking lot of an HBCU. Still, others chose not to read any more into it than they had the other stories.

Acknowledgments

"Planet 4C" was published in *Blind Corner Literary Journal* and won the prize for Afrofuturism Microfiction; "Cold" was published in *A Story In 100 Words*; a version of "Ignominious" was published in *101 Words*; "Junior's Quick Stop" was published in *The Drabble*; a version of "Library Dreams" was published in *50-Word Stories*; and "A Hair Story," "Lonely," and "Searching for Water Where It Never Rains" were published in *The Hampton Renaissance*.

Special thanks to Elle and Zoë for their endless love and support. It is much easier to write when you have a team around you.

Additional thanks to the Dumas Collective (Sabin, Van, and Chris), my parents, Torrey H. Walker, Scott Semegran, Maurice Carlos Ruffin, Rion Amilcar Scott, Grant Faulkner, Matty Dalrymple, Amy Jones, Mitchell Davis, Kelvin Watson, Guy Gonzalez, Tina Rollins, Gladys Bell, Tina McElroy Ansa, the James River Writers, and Dr. Laurie Carter.

Also by Ran Walker

Can I Kick It?: Sneaker Microfiction and Poetry

The Golden Book: A 50-Year Marriage Told In 50-Word Stories

Keep It 100: 100-Word Stories

A Burst of Gray: A Novel In 100-Word Stories

The Library of Afro Curiosities: 100-Word Stories

About the Author

Ran Walker (he/him) is the author of twenty-five books. His short stories, flash fiction, microfiction, and poetry have appeared in a variety of anthologies and journals. Prior to becoming a writer and educator, he worked in magazine publishing and practiced law in Mississippi.

He is the winner of the Indie Author Project's 2019 National Indie Author of the Year Award (selected by judges from *Library Journal, Publishers Weekly*, IngramSpark, St. Martin's Press, and *Writer's Digest*), the 2019 Black Caucus of the American Library Association Best Fiction Ebook Award, the 2018 Virginia Indie Author Project Award for Adult Fiction, and the 2021 Blind Corner Afrofuturism Microfiction Contest. Ran is an Assistant Professor of English and Creative Writing at Hampton University and teaches with Writer's Digest University. He lives in Virginia with his wife and much better half, Lauren, and his amazing "galaxy princess" daughter, Zoë.